The hat is on Gus.

Where is Gus?

Where Is It?

Consultants

Ashley Bishop, Ed.D.

Sue Bishop, M.E.D.

Publishing Credits

Dona Herweck Rice, *Editor-in-Chief*

Robin Erickson, *Production Director*

Lee Aucoin, *Creative Director*

Tim J. Bradley, *Illustrator Manager*

Janelle Bell-Martin, *Illustrator*

Sharon Coan, *Project Manager*

Jamey Acosta, *Editor*

Rachelle Cracchiolo, M.A.Ed., *Publisher*

Teacher Created Materials
5301 Oceanus Drive
Huntington Beach, CA 92649-1030
http://www.tcmpub.com

ISBN 978-1-4333-2942-5

Printed in China WAI002

Where is the hat?

Gus is in the van.

Where is the van?

The van is at the pig pen.

Where is the pig pen?

The pig pen is up the hill.

Where are you?

Glossary

 Gus	 hat
 pig pen	 van

Sight Words

Where is the

on in at

up are you

Extension Activities

Read the story together with your child. Use the discussion questions before, during, and after your reading to deepen your child's understanding of the story and the rime (word family) that is introduced.

The activities provide fun ideas for continuing the conversation about the story and the vocabulary that is introduced. They will help your child make personal connections to the story and use the vocabulary to describe prior experiences.

Discussion Questions

- Who is wearing the hat in the story? Why do people wear hats?
- Where is the van in the story? Who is in the van?
- Where is the pig pen in the story? Where would you find a pig pen?
- Why do you think Gus might have gone to a pig pen?

Activities at Home

- Have your child draw a picture of a pig pen with pigs inside.
- Challenge your child to tell a story the same way it is told in the book but make the words rhyme. Model an example for your child (*Where is Gus? He is on the bus.*).
- Enjoy reading *The Three Little Pigs* with your child.